Dedication

For firefighters everywhere
M.D.B. & C.A.P.

Acknowledgments
The Firefighters of Newton, Massachusetts
Public Education Staff of the
National Fire Protection Association
Roy A. Davis of the
Tacoma, Washington Fire Department
Ruth Landers Glass, SCBWI

Foreword

Fires are scary. The appearance of firefighters can be scary, too. In *Fire Night!* twelve-year-old Katy Wong demonstrates that fire education pays off. Katy applies what she has learned to overcome her fears and make the right decisions.

After pursuing a career as an Air Force pilot, attaining the rank of Colonel, I joined the world of the firefighter. My father had devoted his life to firefighting in New York City. Unlike the simple coat and hat of my father's time, the extensive gear I wear is much more sophisticated. Face masks and air tanks allow maximum protection from smoke and fire.

Not long ago, a newspaper advertisement made me aware of just how terrifying a firefighter in full protective gear can be to a small child. Until then, I had never realized how scary I looked and sounded. I thought that if I were a child, frightened by smoke and fire, the last person I would trust would be a faceless monster, breathing like a nightmare creature. But I know that hiding from this "monster" will ultimately endanger the lives of children and the lives of the firefighters working to save them.

Approximately 1,200 children die in fires in their homes each year. I sincerely hope that reading *Fire Night!* will help to educate your children and reduce this staggering number.

Education is the key. By sharing this book with your children, you will motivate them to listen carefully when fire safety is addressed at school. They may even ask to visit me at the fire house, where they are always welcome.

Roy A. Davis
World Record Holder, Combat Challenge
Tacoma Fire Department
Tacoma, Washington

Katy straightened up her room as she chatted on the phone with her best friend. "It's 8:30 already? I'd better hang up. See you at school tomorrow." Katy's mother popped her head in the doorway.

"Hi, Katy. Dad and I are going for a quick stroll. Your brothers are asleep. We'll be back in twenty minutes."

"Okay, Mom. Have a nice time." Katy heard her parents walk down the stairs and lock the door. She picked up a book and settled herself comfortably in the bean bag chair, pulling a quilt around her. The old radiator in the corner hissed softly.

Enh!! Enh!! Enh!! Enh!! The loud, shrill sound of blaring smoke alarms penetrated the silence. The house was on fire!

Katy jumped to her feet. For a moment, she stood frozen in the middle of her bedroom. Her knees were shaking. She felt sick to her stomach. Thoughts raced through Katy's mind. She had learned about fire safety at school. She knew she had to stay calm and think clearly.

Katy ran to the bedroom door. She felt the door and the doorknob with the back of her hand. Both were cool. She cautiously opened the door and could see her brothers, still asleep in their beds. Katy darted quickly across the hall into her brothers' bedroom, turned on the overhead light, and closed the door behind her.

Kneeling next to her brothers' beds, Katy shook them roughly, flinging off their bed covers. "Sam, wake up! Wake up, Jack!"

"Leave me alone. I'm tired," whined Sam, pushing Katy away and covering his ears.

"Get up! The house is on fire! Hear the smoke alarms?"

Enh!! Enh!! Enh!! Enh!!

"Where's Mom? I want Mom," whimpered Jack.

"Sam, put on your glasses. Come on, Jack. Let's go."

Katy scooped Jack up in her arms and grabbed Sam's hand. Once again, she felt the closed door and doorknob with the back of her hand. Both were cool. She quickly opened the door, headed out of the room and down the hall. Suddenly, the bitter smell of smoke was stronger.

"Sam, get down! Smoke rises. We'll have to crawl."

As they approached the stairs, Katy was stunned by a deafening, cracking sound coming from below. Jack and Sam screamed. The smoke was thicker. Katy's eyes stung and watered. She held her breath and guided the boys back to their bedroom, grabbing the telephone from the hall table. She slammed the door behind her and stuffed a blanket beneath it. Katy ran to the window, unlocked it, and tried to push it open. It stuck. They were trapped.

Katy crouched on the floor, cradling her brothers in her arms. She dialed 911. After the first ring, a woman answered. Katy stuttered at first, but the words spilled out. "I live at 527 School Street in Belmont. My house is on fire! We're on the third floor and we can't get out."

"Okay, stay calm, and don't hang up. What's your name and how old are you?"

"Katy Wong, and I'm twelve."

"Katy, who's there with you?"

"My two brothers. We tried to get out, but the smoke in the hall was too thick. We heard a loud noise from somewhere downstairs. I was afraid to go down."

"Katy, I've called the fire department. You'll hear the sirens in just a minute. Is there a window in the room?"

"Yes, but it's stuck."

Covering the phone with her hand, Katy yelled, "Sam, pull Jack out from under his bed! Don't let him hide!"

"Katy, try the window again."

"Okay." Katy ran to the window. She thumped all four corners of the window frame with her fist, then pushed up against it with the full weight of her body. The window creaked open. Crisp, cold, night air rushed into the room. Katy gulped the clean, invigorating air. She heard sirens blaring. Two fire trucks screeched to a stop in front of the house.

"It opened! The fire trucks are here!" she yelled into the phone.

"Good, Katy. Listen carefully. Find something that's brightly colored, and wave it out the window. Let the firefighters know where you are."

Katy grabbed Sam's yellow bathrobe from his rocking chair and waved it outside.

"Help! Up here! Help!"

One of the firefighters saw Katy and yelled back to her, "We see you! Stay where you are! We're coming up!"

Katy watched the firefighters haul a long ladder to the front of the house. She turned to Sam and Jack. They were both sobbing loudly. The smoke alarms were still blaring. Enh!! Enh!! Enh!! Katy could barely stand the noise.

"Stop crying! It isn't helping anything. The firefighters are here. We'll be okay."

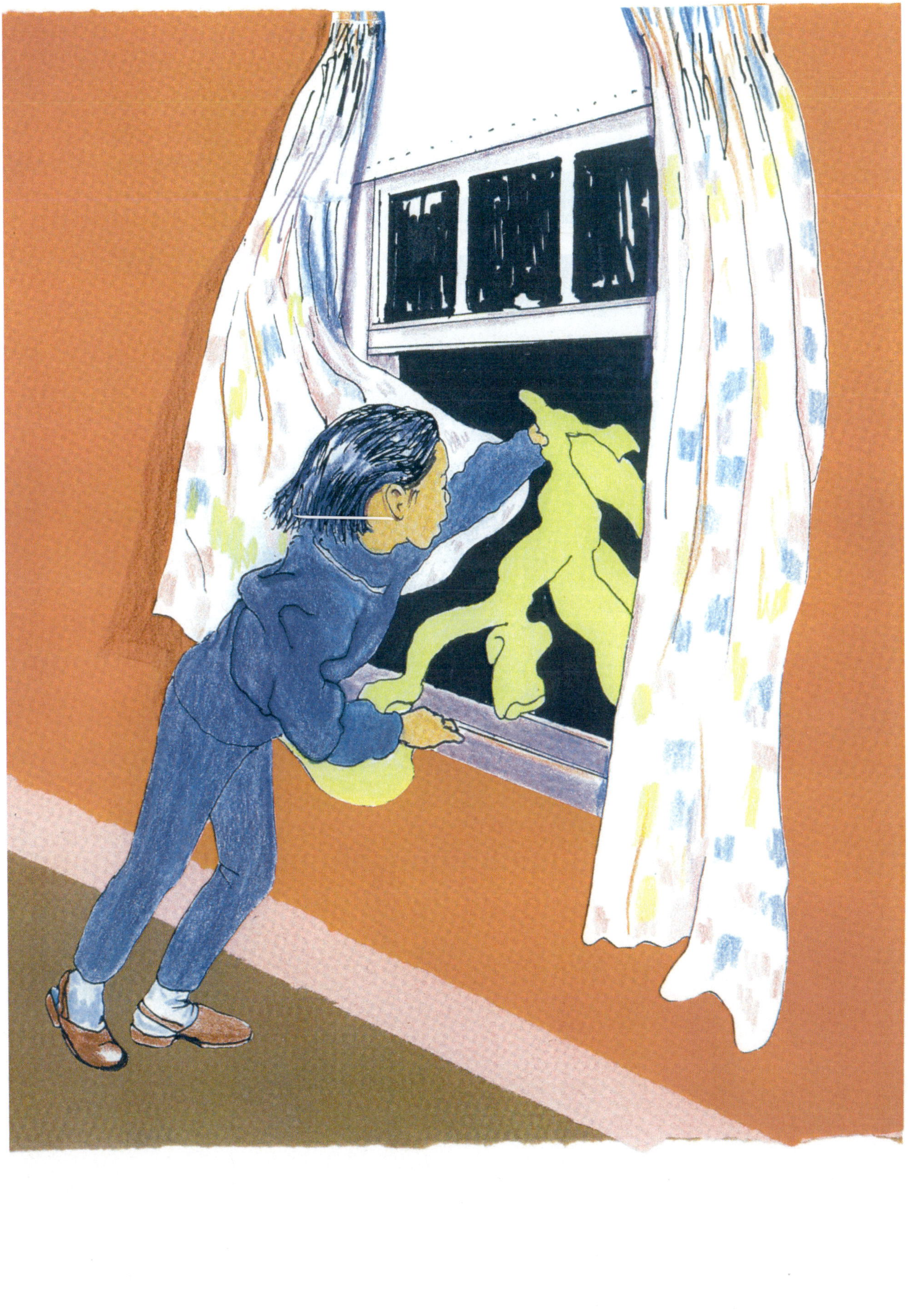

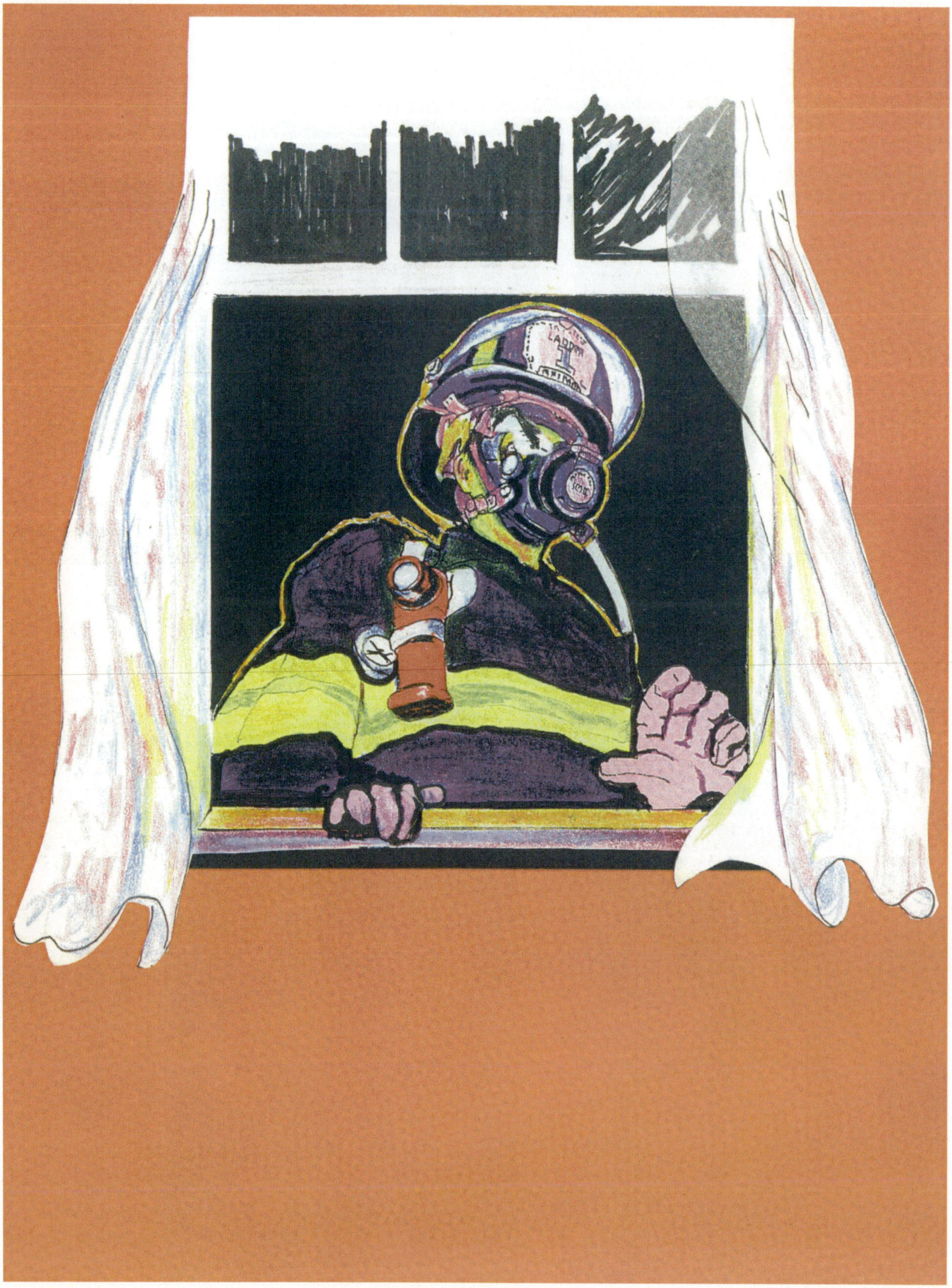

Katy shuddered as the ladder hit the house with a loud thud. Seconds later, the firefighter's dark silhouette appeared at the open window. The firefighter climbed in, breathing noisily through a frightful mask, speaking with a strange, muffled voice. Sam and Jack were terrified. They screamed even louder and shrank away, clinging to their sister.

Katy pulled Jack toward the window. "Come on, Jack. You first. The firefighter's our friend."

The firefighter lifted Jack out the window and handed him to another firefighter, who carried Jack safely to the ground.

"Sam, your turn. You won't get hurt."

As Katy pushed Sam toward the firefighter at the window, Sam whimpered, "Where's Rufus? We can't go without Rufus."

Katy's stomach lurched. How could she have forgotten their dog, Rufus? Why wasn't Rufus barking?

"Hurry, Sam!" came the firefighter's muffled voice from behind the mask. "Let us worry about Rufus."

Finally, it was Katy's turn to climb out the window. With one leg over the windowsill, she glanced at the ground far below. Her stomach flopped. The firefighter's gloved hands steadied her as she stretched her foot toward the ladder. Her foot slipped. She kicked off her shoes. As she backed out the window, still gripping the sill, Katy caught sight of Sam's clock, which had been knocked to the floor — 8:42 p.m. Only minutes had passed since the smoke alarms first sounded. She held the ladder so tightly her knuckles turned white. The firefighters guided her down.

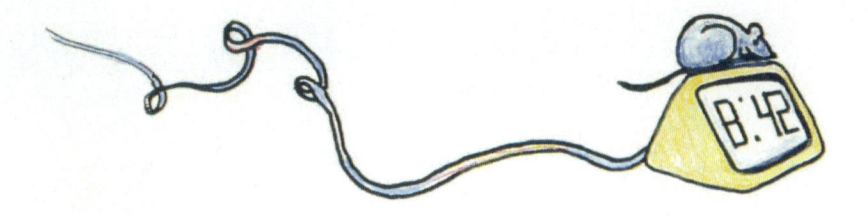

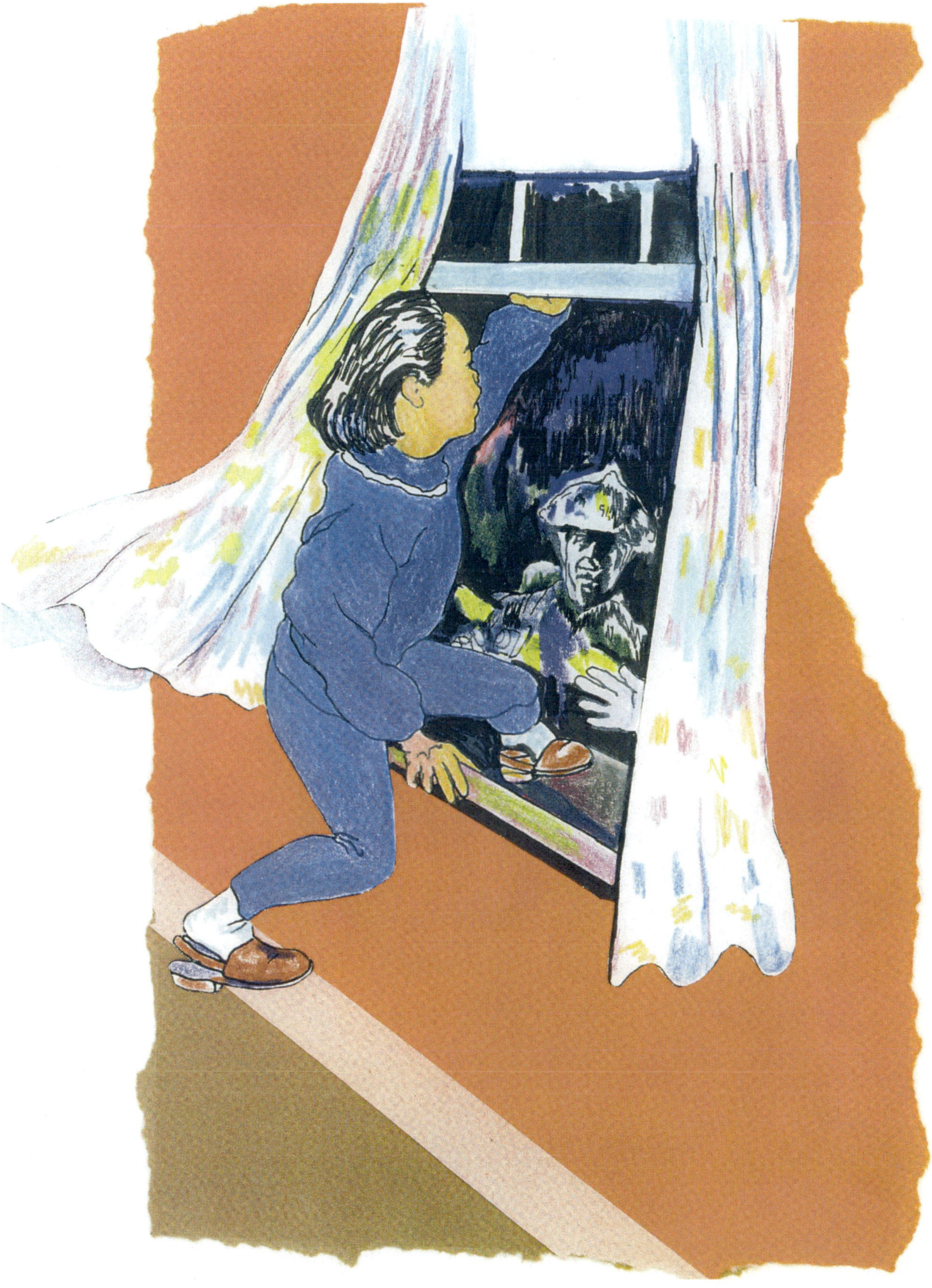

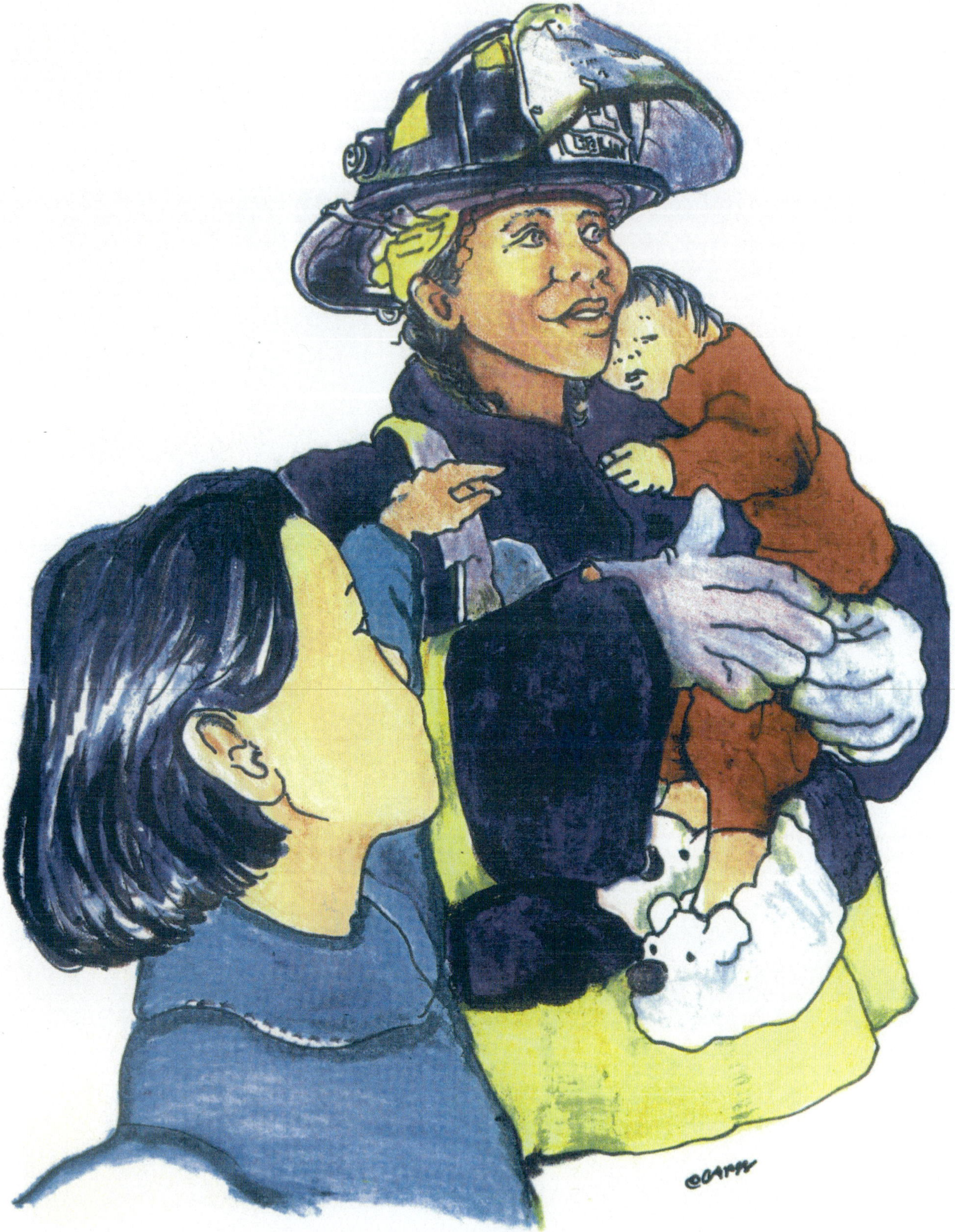

When they were all safely on the ground, the firefighter stood with Katy and the boys, and pulled off the heavy mask. A thick braid fell to the firefighter's shoulder. "You're safe now," she said with a smile.

"Look," blurted Jack. "Our firefighter is a mommy!"

Katy and her brothers stood shivering in the street. A crowd of neighbors formed a protective circle around them. A few minutes later, their parents raced up the street, with Rufus barking at their heels, and charged through the crowd. They hugged their children tightly. Katy hugged back and didn't let go for a long time. The firefighters brought some warm blankets.

The family watched silently as firefighters doused the flames. Finally, the smoke that had billowed through the basement windows disappeared. Katy felt sad and helpless as she stared at the smoldering, soot-streaked house. Scalding tears streamed down her cheeks.

Why did this happen?

As Katy and her family huddled together in the cold, night air, the fire chief approached. "Which one of you is Katy Wong?"

Katy stepped forward. The fire chief shook her hand. "Congratulations, Katy. Thanks to your quick thinking, everyone got out safely. You're a very courageous young woman."

Turning to Katy's parents, the fire chief added, "We'll know more tomorrow about the cause of the fire and the extent of the damages."

Katy huddled with her brothers and Rufus in the back seat of the car as they drove across town to their grandparents' house. The acrid smell of smoke in her hair and on her clothing was sickening. She couldn't stop shaking and shivering.

"Dad is all our stuff ruined?"

"I don't know, Katy. I hope not. I guess we won't know until tomorrow. What's important is that we're all safe."

Early the next morning, Katy's family drove to the fire station. The fire chief explained, "We think the fire was caused when your old furnace overheated and cracked. There was extensive fire damage in the basement. The first and second floors have smoke damage, but you should be able to salvage some of your belongings."

Turning to Katy, the fire chief added, "Katy, there's a newspaper reporter here. She'd like to interview you about the fire. I think people should know how brave you were, and how you helped save your brothers' lives."

When the weekly paper arrived on Thursday, Jack was the first one to notice Katy's photograph. "Look, Katy! You're on the front page."

Katy's father read aloud to the family: "Twelve-year-old Katy Wong, recalling fire safety information she learned at school, acted quickly to save herself and two younger brothers. Finding the stairway from their third-floor bedrooms blocked by smoke, Katy dialed 911. Firefighters arrived quickly on the scene. With their help, all three children escaped unharmed. Cool, calm, and courageous, Katy demonstrated that clear, quick thinking during an emergency can save lives."

Firefighters' Equipment

Helmet

Face Mask

Air Tank

Gloves

Coat

Pants

Boots

Plaster Fork

Flashlight

Axe

FIRE FACTS

Although every emergency situation is different, these fire facts are intended to serve as guidelines, helping you to make the right decisions quickly.

BEFORE A FIRE ...

Learn how to dial 911 (or other emergency number) to report a fire.

Make sure there are smoke alarms on every level, and outside each sleeping area, of your home. They should be cleaned regularly and checked monthly. The batteries should be replaced at least once a year.

With your family, plan and practice an escape route. Know at least two ways out of each room. Choose a safe meeting place outside your home.

Make sure your furnace is professionally cleaned each year.

When in a public place like a school, restaurant, hotel, movie theater, or shopping mall, know where the exits are located.

Help your parents clean out your attic and basement. Don't let trash pile up.

Make sure fire extinguishers are installed in your home. Adults should learn how to use them properly.

DURING A FIRE ...

Don't panic. Stay calm and think clearly.

Never hide in closets or under beds. You cannot hide from fire and smoke.

Get outside as quickly as possible, closing all the doors behind you.

Since smoke and heat rise, stay low and go: Crawl under the smoke to safety.

Feel doors and doorknobs and, if they are warm, do not open. If a door is warm, try to escape through a window.

Call the Fire Department (dial 911 or other emergency number) as soon as you safely can. Once outside, call from a neighbor's phone.

If you cannot escape and are near a phone, call the Fire Department. Hang something light colored (a sheet, towel, or t-shirt) out the window to let firefighters know where you are.

If your clothes catch fire: Stop, drop, and roll. Running only makes the fire burn faster.

Never throw water on a grease or electrical fire. Put a lid (or baking soda or salt) on a grease fire and turn off the burner. For an electrical fire, adults can use a fire extinguisher approved for that purpose.

Do not use elevators. Use stairways to exit.

Never enter a burning building. Call 911 (or other emergency number) and wait for help.

Remember: Firefighters are friends, even though they may look scary.